The Mess Detectives
Case #239:
The Don't-Touchables

Written by Doug Peterson
Illustrated by Ron Eddy & John Trent

BIG IDEA
BOOKS®

zonderkidz

ZONDERVAN.COM/
AUTHORTRACKER

www.bigidea.com

www.zonderkidz.com

Mess Detectives: Case # 239—The Don't-Touchables
Copyright © 2004 by Big Idea Productions
Illustrations copyright © 2004 by Big Idea Productions
Requests for information should be addressed to:
Zonderkidz, Grand Rapids, Michigan 49530

ISBN-10: 0-310-70735-8
ISBN-13: 978-0-310-70735-6

Written by: Doug Peterson
Editors: Cindy Kenney and Gwen Ellis
Illustrations and Design: Big Idea Design
Art Direction: Karen Poth

Printed in China
05 06 07 08 • 6 5 4 3

Be willing to share.
1 Timothy 6:18

Percy Pea doesn't want his little brother to ever touch his stuff. That's why Percy is burning mad. Li'l Pea took Percy's Magnetic Man action figure without even asking! Why can't they just get along? Find out as Detectives Larry and Bob sort through the mess.

Ladies and gentlemen, the story you are about to read is silly. The names have been changed to protect the serious.

This is a city where messes are made and messes are cleaned up. I should know. I'm a mess detective. My name is Detective Larry the Cucumber, and my partner is Bob the Tomato. He carries a badge. I carry a badger.

Don't ask why.

11:23 a.m.

I was drawing doodles in my notepad when a call came in from the 45th precinct. Percy Pea was in a mess. A big mess. And he needed our help. So Bob and I leaped into our police car and raced to the north side of Bumblyburg.

When we reached his house, we found Percy in his room, looking really mad. "What seems to be the trouble?" Bob asked Percy Pea.

"My little brother has been messing with my things," he grumbled.

"Mm-hmm," I said. I really have a way with words.

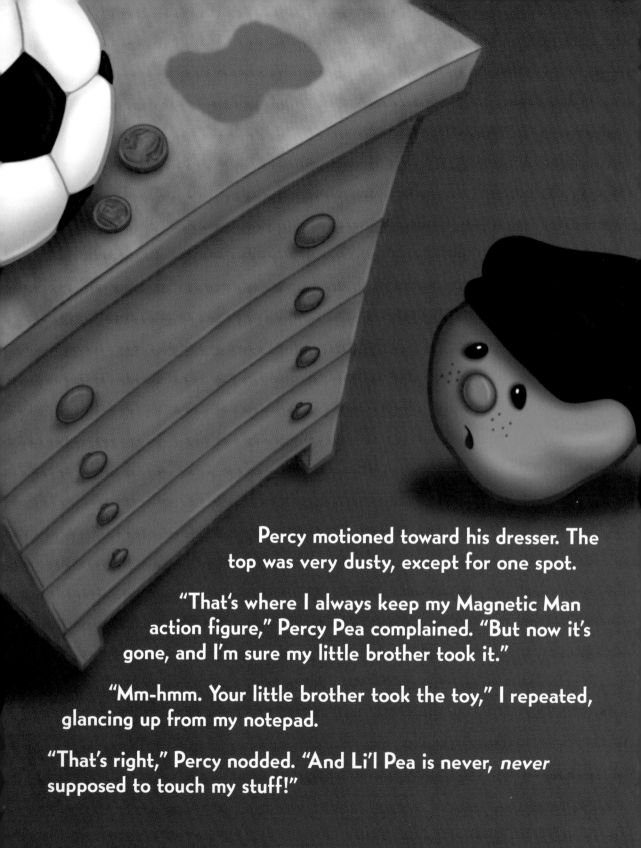

Percy motioned toward his dresser. The top was very dusty, except for one spot.

"That's where I always keep my Magnetic Man action figure," Percy Pea complained. "But now it's gone, and I'm sure my little brother took it."

"Mm-hmm. Your little brother took the toy," I repeated, glancing up from my notepad.

"That's right," Percy nodded. "And Li'l Pea is never, *never* supposed to touch my stuff!"

"Then that makes you a Don't-Touchable," I pointed out.

"A *what?*" asked Percy.

"A Don't-Touchable. That's someone who doesn't like it when people touch his stuff. I should know. My former partner was always borrowing my things. His name was Elliot Mess, and he kept messing with my notepad. It was very upsetting. He even took—"

"Larry?" Bob said.

"Yes, Bob?"

"Can we just stick to *this* case?"

"Sure thing, Bob."

I have to forget the past. What's done is done. Life goes on.

1:35 p.m.

After putting out a police alert for the missing action figure, we called Percy Pea down to the station to view a line-up. Ten different Magnetic Man action figures were lined up against the wall in a special room. Percy looked at them from behind a two-way mirror.

"Are any of these action figures your missing toy?" Bob asked.

"Take your time," I encouraged. "We need a positive I.D." I wasn't sure what "positive I.D." meant, but it sounded good. Really good.

Percy slowly shook his head. "None of these are my missing toy. My action figure had its arm broken off."

I looked up in shock. "You mean we're looking for a one-armed toy?" I asked.

"Well... ya," said Percy.

"How did your toy get broken?" asked Bob.

"Li'l Pea broke his arm off last week," Percy explained.
"That's why I never let him touch my things!"

"Elliot Mess broke one of my things once," I recalled, sadly. The memory stung. "He took my pencil without asking, and he busted it! After that, I asked for a new partner, and we haven't spoken since. That's also when I became a Don't-Touchable. I went on daring raids, barging into houses to stop kids from messing with their brother's and sister's stuff. I couldn't forget how Elliot had taken my—"

"Larry?"

"Yes, Bob?"

"You're getting off the subject again," he said.

"You're right. I have to put the past behind me. It's water under the bridge." I wasn't sure what "water under the bridge" meant, but it sounded good. Really good.

2:46 p.m.

We were called back to the Pea house, where a 415—an argument—was in progress. Things were getting ugly.

"Hello, ma'am," I said to Mrs. Pea. "My name is Larry the Cucumber, and this is my partner, Bob the Tomato. He carries a badge. I carry a badger. Don't ask why."

"What seems to be the trouble?" Bob asked.

Mrs. Pea began telling
us about how the pea brothers grew up.

"Just the facts, ma'am," Bob told her.

"Percy and Li'l Pea are fighting over everything in their
room," she said. "They won't share *anything*!"

I made a note of that.

What we found
when we entered the
bedroom was shocking! Percy had
run a strip of yellow crime tape down the
middle of the room, right between the twin beds.

"What's going on here?" Bob asked Percy.

"I'm dividing our room in half," he said. "Li'l Pea stays on his side of the room, and I stay on my side. That way, he won't be touching my things. If he isn't touching my things, he won't be breaking them."

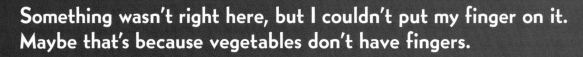

Something wasn't right here, but I couldn't put my finger on it. Maybe that's because vegetables don't have fingers.

"Percy blames *me* because his action figure is missing," Li'l Pea moaned. "But I never took it."

"You mean you're innocent?" Bob clarified.

"Yes!"

"But you did break the arm off his toy last week. Am I right about that?" I asked.

"No!" Li'l Pea shouted. "Did he say I broke his Magnetic Man action figure?"

"Yep," I answered.

"That's not true!" Li'l Pea protested.

"Is too!" shouted Percy.

"I was playing with his toy last week," Li'l Pea said. "I admit that. But when Percy saw me playing with it, he got mad and grabbed it away from me. *That's* how it got broken!"

I made a note of that.

The pieces of the puzzle were beginning to fall into place.

Bob turned to face Percy. "Is this true?"

"Well—yes it is—" Percy was at a loss for words. "But that still doesn't give him the right to mess with my stuff."

He was right about that. Section 3.5, Paragraph 29 of the Messy Code made it very clear.

"My toy is gone, and it's *his* fault!" Percy said.

"You mean *this* toy?" asked Li'l Pea.

While we were talking, Li'l Pea had crawled behind Percy's dresser. He came out carrying the Magnetic Man action figure, which was covered in dust bunnies; as was Li'l Pea.

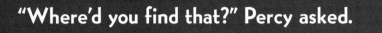

"Where'd you find that?" Percy asked.

"Under the dresser. It must have fallen behind it."

Percy was stunned. He had never thought to look under his dresser. He was so sure that Li'l Pea had messed with his toy.

"Percy, don't you see what's happening?" Bob pointed out. "You won't share with your brother. And when people don't share, things get broken."

"You mean like my toy's arm?" Percy said.

"Not just that," Bob explained. "When people don't share, they break apart friendships. Sharing brings people together."

Percy stared at the floor, deep in thought. I was feeling pretty lousy myself. I couldn't stop thinking about my old friend, Elliot Mess.

"What do you think about what I just said?" Bob asked Percy.

Suddenly, I couldn't take it anymore. "I'm sorry!" I shouted, beginning to sob. I pulled out my handkerchief. "I know I should have shared my stuff! You're right, man! You're so right!"

Bob looked at me in shock. So did Percy and Li'l Pea. Even my badger seemed startled.

"What does any of this have to do with you, Larry?" asked Bob.

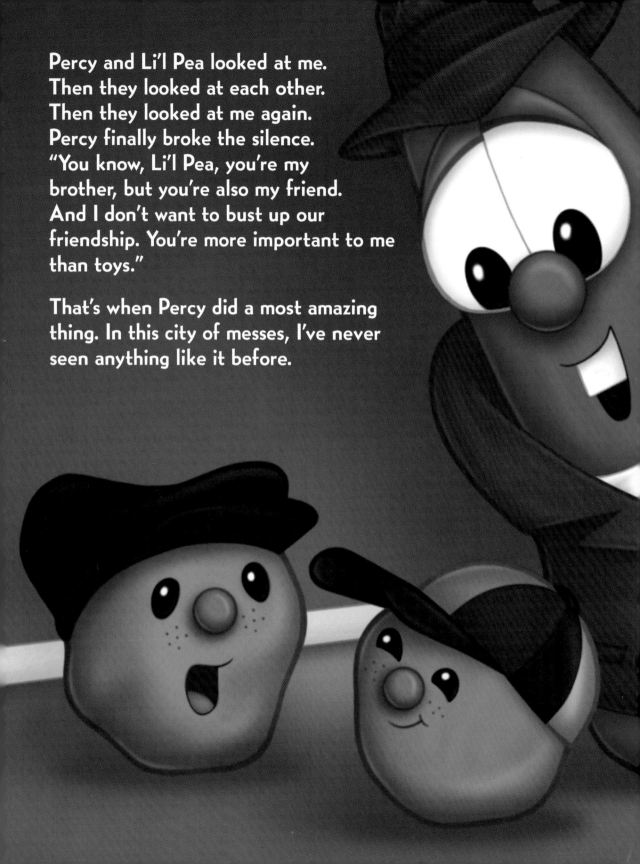

Percy and Li'l Pea looked at me.
Then they looked at each other.
Then they looked at me again.
Percy finally broke the silence.
"You know, Li'l Pea, you're my
brother, but you're also my friend.
And I don't want to bust up our
friendship. You're more important to me
than toys."

That's when Percy did a most amazing
thing. In this city of messes, I've never
seen anything like it before.

He tore down the yellow
crime scene tape that separated
his half of the room from Li'l Pea's
half. Then he said, "I'm sorry." Two
little words. But they did big things.

3:15 p.m.

When we left the scene of the crime, Percy and Li'l Pea were having a great time together. They were sharing their toys. And as they shared, they became closer than ever. It was almost as if sharing drew them together like a magnet. Magnetic men—or magnetic peas, in this case.

Meanwhile, I was on the car phone to my old partner, Elliot Mess. I told him I was sorry for becoming a Don't-Touchable. To my surprise, he said he was sorry, too. He said he shouldn't have borrowed my things without asking.

"10-4," I said to Elliot just before I hung up the car phone. I wasn't sure what "10-4" meant, but it sounded good. Really good.

Then I turned to Bob, who was trying to yank
his badge out of my badger's teeth.

"Say, Bob?"

"Yes, Larry."

"Any time you need to borrow my notepad, just say the word. You can use it."

"Thanks, good buddy."

I smiled a big, toothy grin. I knew what "good buddy" meant, and it sounded good. Really good.